SHONEN JUMP'S

Yu-Gi-Oh! GX

UNDEFEATED HERO

D0628051

SHONEN JUMP'S

Yu-Gi-Oh! GX

UNDEFEATED HERO

Adapted by Tracey West

SCHOLASTIC INC.

New York Toronto London Auckland Sydney
Mexico City New Delhi Hong Kong Buenos Aires

ISBN-13: 978-0-439-88833-2
ISBN-10: 0-439-88833-6

Published by Scholastic Inc.
SCHOLASTIC and associated logos are trademarks and/or registered
trademarks of Scholastic Inc.

12 11 10 9 8 7 6 5 4 3 2 1   7 8 9 10 11 12/0

Designed by Phil Falco
Printed in the U.S.A.
First printing, March 2007

UNDEFEATED HERO

CHAPTER ONE

ENTER THE ADMIRAL

"You did what?!" Syrus Truesdale yelled. His pale eyes were wide with disbelief behind his glasses. "So then where am I going to sleep?"

Syrus sat across from his friend Jaden Yuki in the dining hall of the Slifer Red dorm. Jaden leaned back in his chair, looking as relaxed as he always did.

"I'm sorry," he said. "I guess in all the excitement I didn't think about that."

"Excitement!" Syrus was really screaming now. "You traded my bed for a *card*!"

The other diners stopped eating and looked at Syrus and Jaden. Jaden was notorious around Duel Academy for doing outrageous things, but trading your friend's bed for a Duel Monsters card was pretty unbelievable.

"But I got it for you," Jaden explained. "Isn't your birthday next week?"

"It was last Tuesday!" Syrus cried. "And I'm surprised I made it, with everything you put me through this year. I may need a new roommate."

"Don't say that!" Jaden said. "I'm really sorry, Syrus! I promise I'll be the best roommate from now on!"

A few tables away, a student in a black uniform laughed out loud. "What's this? Trouble in paradise?" Chazz Princeton joked.

Syrus frowned. "Hey! This is private!"

"Come on, it's just Chazz!" Jaden said cheerfully. He walked over to Chazz's table. "We share everything, you know. Like dessert!"

Chazz pulled his lunch plate away. "Yeah right, Slifer Slacker!" he sneered. "Keep dreaming!"

"Okay," Jaden said. "Then can I have your corn dogs, too? And your mashed potatoes?"

"How about asking for a bed while you're at it?" Syrus snapped.

Before Jaden could reply, Chumley Huffington, Jaden and Syrus's roommate, ran into the dining hall.

"Anyone order a sub?" he asked.

Jaden shrugged, confused. Did Chumley mean a submarine sandwich?

"Because there's one parked outside!" Chumley finished.

"Say what?" Jaden cried. A real submarine! He had to see that.

Minutes later, he was standing on the shores of Academy Island. Most of the academy's students had gathered there to see the sub. Jaden's friends Alexis, from the Obelisk Blue dorm, and Bastion, from the Ra Yellow dorm, had followed him, Syrus, and Chazz to the end of the dock to see what was going on.

A huge gray submarine floated offshore. Standing on

the deck was a burly man wearing a purple jacket, a striped shirt, and white pants. A white captain's hat sat on his head, and bushy sideburns covered his face. He held a microphone in his hand.

"Avast, ye landlubbers!" the man cried in a booming voice. "I be the Admiral!"

"Is he like a pirate or something?" Jaden wondered.

The Admiral seemed insulted. "Ye scallywags never laid ears on the tales of the Admiral? Scourge of the seven seas?"

"Um, yeah, I'm thinking he's a pirate," Alexis said.

"I set sail to challenge one of ye to a duel!" the Admiral bellowed. The crowd gasped. "The bilge rat Jaden Yuki!"

◆ CHAPTER TWO ◆

GET YAARR GAME ON!

A chill went through Jaden and his friends.

Bastion and Chazz stared at the Admiral. "Is he . . ."

"A Shadow Rider!" Jaden exclaimed.

In the last few weeks, Jaden and his friends had experienced incredible danger facing duelists known as the Shadow Riders. Beneath Duel Academy, two Sacred Beasts had been locked up for ages. Once unlocked, they could destroy the world. The Shadow Riders were trying to obtain the seven keys needed to release the beasts — but to get the keys, they had to challenge the Key Keepers, the seven best duelists at Duel Academy.

Jaden, Bastion, Chazz, and Alexis were all Key Keepers. Syrus's brother, Zane, and Professor Banner and Professor Crowler rounded out the team. So far, Professor

Crowler, Zane, and Bastion had all lost their keys. Jaden had dueled three Shadow Riders and won — but nearly lost his life in the process.

In his most recent battle, Jaden faced off against a tough Amazoness named Tania. She'd already taken Bastion's Spirit Key, and was on the hunt for more! It was a close duel, but in the end, Jaden's Elemental Hero Wildheart triumphed over Tania's Amazoness Swordswoman and Jaden kept the Sacred Beast cards safe once more.

Tania and all the other Shadow Riders had appeared without warning, just like the Admiral.

"Show yourself, Jaden!" the sailor called out. "Where ye be?"

"Ye be here!" Jaden called back, stepping forward. "Aren't you a little old to be playing dress-up?"

The Admiral's face flushed with anger. "At arms, ye scurvy dog!" he challenged. "We be dueling! Get yaaaaaarr game on!"

"Now?" Jaden cried, surprised.

"No, next week," Bastion said drily.

"This should be good!" Chazz said.

Jaden hesitated. Each shadow duel he had fought had been more painful and difficult than the last. He wasn't afraid, but . . .

"Ye best come aboard!" the Admiral threatened. "If not, I be tying yer mates to the yardarm for Davy Jones!"

That did it. No one threatened Jaden's friends. He marched forward.

"Jaden, hold up!" Alexis cried. "If this is a Shadow Game, no way we're letting you go all alone. I'm coming with you."

Jaden frowned. "I don't know. Syrus had a point," he said. "In all my duels lately, my friends always end up in danger."

Jaden's mind flashed back to his duel with

Nightshroud. The Shadow Rider had held Syrus and Chumley hostage over a pit of bubbling lava!

But Alexis was not afraid. "Jaden, we're in this together," she said firmly.

"Right! I'm with you, too," Bastion said.

Chazz stepped forward. "Just wish I had a parrot. Or an eye patch."

"That settles it!" Alexis said.

"*Aaaaar!*" the Admiral said impatiently. "I'll scuttle the likes of ya, 'less ye come aboard!"

Jaden turned to Syrus, who stood next to Chumley, his eyes facing the ground.

"So, Syrus, are you gonna come?" Jaden asked.

But Syrus couldn't answer. He shuffled his feet and avoided Jaden's gaze.

Jaden sighed. He wanted his best friend with him. But at least he wasn't going alone.

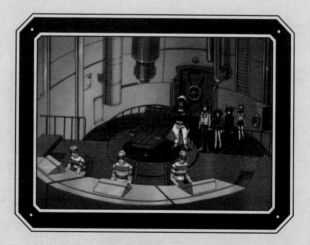

The Admiral sent a small speedboat to the dock to fetch Jaden and his friends. They sped across the water toward the large submarine. Once they climbed on deck, they walked onto a small square platform with the Admiral.

The platform descended into the sub's high-tech control room. Several crewmen in striped shirts manned computers and machines around the room. A window in the control room looked out upon an underwater dueling arena contained in a glass dome. There was a flat circular platform at each end of the arena for each duelist to stand on. A long pipe stretched across the field between the platforms.

"High tech, for a pirate," Bastion remarked. "I'm beginning to think this admiral is less buccaneer and more financier. How else could he afford a submarine or a submerged duel arena?"

Jaden was impressed. "Whoa, check this out! Talk about shiver me timbers!"

"*Aaaar*, this be a fine ship!" the Admiral agreed. "But let's weigh anchor and duel! Wish your mates farewell. You ain't be seein' them again!"

⬦ CHAPTER THREE ⬦

AN UNFRIENDLY WAGER

"What are you waiting for, Admiral? Are we gonna duel, or walk the plank?" Jaden taunted.

The Admiral activated his Duel Disk, which was encrusted with gleaming jewels.

"At arms, ye grog-snarfin' swine!" the Admiral cried.

"Sure! Whatever that means!" Jaden called back. "Duel!"

Jaden took five cards from his Duel Disk. He examined them, then quickly held up one.

"I summon Elemental Hero Wildheart in defense mode!" he said.

A life-size holographic image of the card appeared next to Jaden. Wildheart was a muscled warrior with long black hair and a loincloth. He had 1600 defense points.

Suddenly, the duel arena went dark.

"Shoulda guessed you'd turn off all the lights," Jaden said. "It *is* a Shadow Game!"

"A Shadow Game?" The Admiral seemed confused.

"What's it for? My soul? My key?" Jaden asked. "Are 'ye' gonna turn me into a doll, or maybe suck me into some magic card?"

"What yer tongue be spoutin'?" the Admiral asked. "'Tis no Shadow Game!"

"But what about my key?" Jaden asked.

"Key? What key?" the Admiral replied.

"The key that —" Jaden began, then stopped. Maybe the Admiral was telling the truth. "You *are* trying to unlock the Spirit Gates, right? Aren't you?"

"Why, ye scrappy swine, I'm no Shadow Rider, and I'll prove it!" the Admiral bellowed. "Bring a spring upon 'er cable and let's careen this lady sky bound!"

The submarine lurched as the crew obeyed the Admiral's orders. The sub broke through the top of the water into the sunshine.

"This guy sure knows his sailing," Alexis remarked. "Guess he's really not a Shadow Rider!"

"If this isn't a Shadow Game, how did he shroud the duel arena in darkness?" Bastion wondered.

Just then, a sailor walked into the control room and addressed another crewman.

"Sir, we've fixed the lights in the arena!"

Alexis and Bastion groaned.

Back in the duel arena, Jaden and the Admiral faced off.

"See, me mate? I'm an Ocean Rider, not some son of a sprog Shadow Rider!" the Admiral said.

"Hey, whatever you say, Cappy," Jaden shrugged.

"I be an Admiral!" the sailor corrected him. "And

now, let's duel! Prepare to taste the briny deep with this — Legendary Ocean!"

The Admiral held up a card, and immediately the duel arena looked like the bottom of the ocean. Seawater swirled around them, and ocean plants and stone walls rose from the sandy floor. Jaden panicked.

"I can't breathe!" he cried.

His friends watched from the control room.

"Jaden, you do realize that you're not drowning," Bastion reminded him over the intercom. "It's just a hologram!"

"Oh yeah!" Jaden relaxed. "Maybe they'll throw in some holographic lobsters for lunch!"

The Admiral didn't appreciate Jaden's joking. "Will ye think it be a grand laugh when me sea monsters rip ye limb from limb, matey?"

"What?" Jaden asked. That didn't sound good.

The Admiral grinned. "The field spell I just cast reduces the summoning level of all Water Attribute Monsters," he explained. "Meaning I can play Orca Mega-Fortress of Darkness without a sacrifice! And I'll be doing just that!"

The Admiral held up the card, and the water in the arena began to churn as a huge black and white whale appeared on the field. Orca had sharp teeth, a helmet on its huge head, and 2100 attack points.

"But don't be forgettin' that me sea monsters be gettin' an extra bounty of 200 points for attackin' or defendin'!" the Admiral bragged. Orca's attack points jumped to 2300.

"Now, me Orca Mega-Fortress, scuttle Wildheart!"

the Admiral cried. He looked at Jaden. "That means attack, ye swab!"

Orca opened its massive mouth to reveal a big cannon. A yellow ball of light shot from the cannon and tore through the water, crashing into Wildheart. The hero didn't have enough defense points to withstand the attack, and it vanished from the field. Jaden cried out as a huge wave washed over him.

"I be expectin' more from you, Jaden," the Admiral said. "I know who ye be. Yer deck. Yer victories. Oh, yes. I've studied ya like a map! Which is why I came to find ye! Oh, and I lays a facedown."

"Me? Why?" Jaden asked. But there was no time for questions. They were in the middle of a duel. "While you think on that, I summon Elemental Hero Avian in defense mode!"

The hero, with his large white wings, appeared on the field with 1000 defense points.

"And I'll be throwin' down a facedown," Jaden said. "So, what's so important about me? Hmm? Why'd you go to all this trouble?"

"Well, lad, the Admiral's to be buildin' a new duel academy at the bottom of the briny deep," he explained. "But thar be a hitch! Me still need a first mate. A mate who be grand. A mate like . . . ye!" He pointed at Jaden. "And you'll help me run it, ye swab!" the Admiral announced.

Jaden's friends watched and listened.

"Not Jaden! He can't leave us!" Alexis cried.

"Why not? It's an amazing opportunity," Bastion pointed out.

"Good. Maybe now I'll get a new room," Chazz added.

"Jaden, ye be the finest duelist on the seven seas," the Admiral continued. "I want ye to teach with me. Ye'd be great."

"It's true," Jaden admitted. "I mean, I *have* taught Chazz a few things."

"Then ye're in!" the Admiral said quickly. "Welcome aboard!"

"I was joking," Jaden protested.

"Well then, what do ye say to a friendly wager 'tween mates?" the Admiral asked.

"Forget it!" Jaden replied.

"I ain't be askin' ye," the Admiral said darkly. "I be tellin'! The duel has begun and them wagers be backed by bone! If ye win, I'll be letting ye and yer mates go free. But if not, ye leave Duel Academy and join me!"

The Admiral's cruel laugh echoed through the duel arena.

Jaden glared at the Admiral, his mind resolved.

He had to win now. Losing just wasn't an option.

· CHAPTER FOUR ·

LEVIA-DRAGON DAEDALUS!

"My turn," the Admiral said. "And I play a trap known as Cursed Waters Level 3!"

"Wicked name," Jaden said. "But what does it do?"

"It be lettin' me summon monsters from the deep whose levels total three!" the Admiral bragged. "And me be summoning Torpedo Fish and Cannonball Spear Shellfish!"

Two monsters appeared on the field in front of the sailor. Torpedo Fish looked like a large pointy fish with shiny green and silver scales. Cannonball Spear Shellfish was all shining silver metal, with a body like a thick corkscrew that came to a sharp point at the end. Both monsters had an attack level of 1000, which rose to 1200 thanks to the Legendary Ocean field card.

Bastion watched from the control room, impressed.

He quickly did the math in his head. Torpedo Fish normally had a summoning level of 3, and Cannonball Spear Shellfish had a summoning level of 2. But . . .

"Brilliant! Thanks to the card Legendary Ocean, both of their levels decrease by one, resulting in a new total of three. Clever," Bastion said. That meant the Admiral could use Cursed Waters Level 3 to summon them both.

"And now I be activatin' the special ability of the fierce Orca of Darkness," the Admiral continued, "by sendin' one of me beasts to Davy Jones's, so mees can scuttle your facedown."

Jaden didn't know much pirate talk, but he figured out that the Admiral was going to sacrifice one of his cards so Jaden would lose a facedown.

That's exactly what happened. Cannonball Spear Shellfish hurtled through the water at Jaden, exploding at

the last minute. Jaden's facedown card shattered at the same moment. Jaden groaned.

"Thar be more," the Admiral warned. "I be biddin' adieu to me fish to make your green feathered fellow walk the mutinous plank!"

Jaden frowned. Another sacrifice — and another card lost for Jaden!

Torpedo Fish sped across the field and slammed into Elemental Hero Avian. Both cards exploded in a flash, then were gone. Jaden was defenseless.

"*Har har har!*" the Admiral chuckled. "Now me orca has a clear line of sight. Fire!"

The orca's gigantic mouth opened wide once again, and another blast of yellow flame burst from the cannon inside. This time, the blast hit Jaden directly, along with a forceful tidal wave. The impact of the attack knocked Jaden to his knees. His life points dropped from 4000 down to 1700.

"Oh no!" Bastion cried, worried.

But Jaden lifted up his head and grinned.

"Not bad!" Jaden said. "Haven't gotten that wet since the walrus show at Sea Land."

"'Tis no theme park!" the Admiral growled.

"It could be. You just need some rides," Jaden joked. He pulled a card from his Duel Disk. "Maybe something like this!"

Jaden held up the card Polymerization. It had helped him out many times in the past, allowing him to summon two monsters and then fuse them into a more powerful creature.

"Just watch as Polymerization takes Clayman and

Sparkman for a spin to make Elemental Hero Thunder Giant!" Jaden cried.

A hero in golden armor appeared on the field. On his chest was a glowing orb. Jagged lightning flashed inside the orb, and he had 2400 attack points.

"Is that the best ye got, mate?" the Admiral taunted. "Even if thar yellow-bellied gizzard keelhauls me orca, me only take a mere hundred points of damage, ya salty swab!"

Jaden grinned. "Ya missed the boat, Admiral," he said. "Let me fill ya in! When I summoned my Thunder Giant, he automatically destroys one monster with fewer attack points than he has."

The Admiral looked shocked. "How that be?"

Jaden shrugged. "I read the card," he said. "Now, Thunder Giant, let's reel that whale in. Static Blast!"

A fierce lightning bolt shot from the orb on Thunder

Giant's chest. It pierced the orca, shattering the giant beast. The Admiral cried out.

"And now, Thunder Giant attacks you directly!" Jaden cried. "Voltic Thunder!"

Thunder Giant hurled a ball of growling thunder at the Admiral.

"Shiver me timbers!" he screamed. The force of the attack knocked him to his knees. His life points dropped from 4000 to 1600.

But Jaden wasn't done yet. "And I'll throw a couple of facedowns," he said. "It's your move."

"*Aaaaar!*" The sailor rose to his feet with a groan. "Perchance a deal. We maroon this duel here and now and you come work for me for a thousand doubloons."

Jaden's friends all gasped.

"How much?" Chazz asked in disbelief.

"That's over a million dollars!" Bastion exclaimed.

"What say ye, Jaden?" the Admiral asked. "Do ye want to be rich?"

"Nope," Jaden said firmly. His friends groaned. "Don't you get it? I don't care about the money."

"But what else have ye back at Duel Academy?" the Admiral pointed out. "Yer mate Syrus doesn't want ye. Mull it over whilst we duel. But remember, if I win, you'll be mine either way."

The Admiral held up a card. "And now, me play this: the Shallow Grave!"

Jaden frowned. He had never seen that card before.

"Here's how the card works," the Admiral explained.

"We search our graveyards and find a beast we want, then summon it in defense mode. Think I'll be choosin' the terror of the seven seas: the Orca Mega-Fortress of Darkness!"

The giant whale appeared on the field once again.

"And I'll bring back Clayman," Jaden announced.

The sturdy hero appeared on the field. Jaden knew his 2000 defense points would come in handy.

The Admiral didn't look worried. "Before yer Thunder Giant makes quick work o' me orca, I be tellin' ya he's just a sacrifice! So hold on to your britches, for thar be another monster, and he be called Levia-Dragon Daedalus!"

Orca vanished in a flash of light. The waters churned as a huge sea serpent appeared in its place. It was twice as huge as Orca, with sharp fangs in its large mouth. It let out a roar that seemed to shake the sub. Its attack points rose from 2600 to 2800 due to the Legendary Ocean card in effect.

"Whoa," Jaden said, impressed. "Nice fish. Does he bite?"

"Ye best be worried 'bout his special ability," the Admiral warned. "By sendin' me Legendary Ocean to the graveyard, the whole lot o' cards on this here field o' war meet a dastardly end!"

The Admiral sacrificed the field card, and the duel arena returned to its normal state. Levia-Dragon's attack points dropped back down to 2600.

Jaden quickly made a move. "Before it's too late, I'll use Emergency Provisions!" he cried, turning up his face-down. "I just kick a trap or spell card over to the graveyard and my life points get . . . a big one-triple-zero!"

Jaden sacrificed his other facedown card, and his life points jumped from 1700 to 2700 in a flash.

"'Tis of no matter!" the Admiral scoffed. "'Cause yer cards be goin' the way of Davy Jones!"

A white-hot ball of light burst from Levia-Dragon's

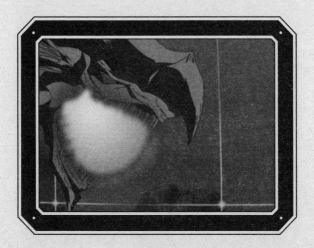

mouth, slamming into Thunder Giant and Clayman. They both vanished from the field.

"Attack!" the Admiral yelled.

Levia-Dragon hurled a ball of blue light directly at Jaden. He shielded his face from the blast. His life points dropped way, way down — only 100 left.

"He's done," Chazz said.

"Jaden!" Alexis cried.

The Admiral laughed. "Ye be *my* treasure now!"

• CHAPTER FIVE •

BUBBLE BLASTER TO THE RESCUE!

"Yar be finished!" the Admiral crowed. "Ain't nothin' ye can do to stop me monster!"

"We'll just see about that," Jaden said, gritting his teeth. "I got one draw left, mate. It's all or nothin'. Here we go!"

Jaden's friends all held their breath as Jaden drew his card.

"I special summon Elemental Hero Bubbleman!" he cried. The hero had a pale blue uniform with blue armor strapped across his thick chest. A white cape hung down his back. Best of all, he had 800 attack points.

The Admiral grunted. "What be so special?"

"I'll tell ya!" Jaden said. "Bubbleman hates being alone, so when he's the last card in my hand I get to special summon him automatically. And if he's the only card on the field when he makes his big appearance, I get to draw two more cards from my deck!"

"Blast!" the Admiral cried.

Jaden drew two cards from his Duel Disk. He grinned and held up one of them.

"I now activate Pot of Greed," he said. "That gives me two more cards!"

"Ye swine!" The Admiral shook his fist as Jaden drew two more cards.

"Then I'll play this guy," Jaden continued. "The Warrior Returning Alive brings back one warrior monster from my graveyard."

"I'll be hornswoggled!" the Admiral exclaimed.

"Welcome back, Sparkman!" Jaden announced. The blue and gold hero appeared back on the field, with 1600 attack points. The Admiral growled.

"There's more," Jaden said. "I play the spell Metamorphosis. All I've got to do is sacrifice one of my monsters, and I get to summon a fusion monster of the same level. So say hello to Elemental Hero Neo Bubbleman!"

Jaden sacrificed Bubbleman, and a new hero appeared in his place. Neo Bubbleman had the same number of attack points — 800 — but he was sleeker, with powerful white wings.

"Then I'll play this," Jaden continued. "The equip spell Bubble Blaster, for a sweet bonus of 800 attack points."

Neo Bubbleman's attack points rose to 1600, and a cannon-shaped weapon appeared in his arms.

"Neo, turn that fish into a sushi special!" Jaden commanded. "Bubble Slamming Stream!"

A powerful jet of water burst from the Bubble Blaster. It hit Levia-Dragon directly in the face — but nothing much happened.

"*Aaaaar, haar haar!*" the Admiral laughed. "Ye daft? Me sea monster has more points than yer bubble boy! Try again, ye salty swab!"

"If you insist," Jaden said. "By sacrificing my Bubble Blaster, I reduce your damage to zero!"

The Bubble Blaster disappeared, and Neo Bubbleman's attack points dropped back to 800.

"And Neo Bubbleman has a surprise of his own," Jaden went on. "See, after the damage is dealt, your dragon goes boom!"

The Levia-Dragon exploded in a flash of blinding light and fiery flame.

"Sweet effect, don't you think?" Jaden said. "And, Admiral, you haven't forgotten about my Sparkman, have you?"

"*Aaar!*" the Admiral cried. He knew what was coming.

"Sparkman, shiver his timbers!" Jaden cried.

The hero assaulted the Admiral directly with a barrage of light. The Admiral cried out and fell to the platform. His life points dropped to zero.

"That's game!" Jaden cried happily.

The Admiral looked at the floor, pretending to be upset. Instead, he smiled a wicked grin.

"I might have been bested in this here duel, but thar be another way to catch this wily fish Jaden," he said under his breath.

The Admiral had been hatching his plan all along. When

he and Jaden returned to the control room, Jaden's friends were missing.

"What do you mean, they left?" Jaden asked in disbelief.

"They took the first and only dinghy home," the Admiral said.

"So I'm stuck?" Jaden asked.

"See for yerself," the sailor replied. "High-def video tells no tall tales."

Jaden watched on the control room screens. Alexis, Bastion, and Chazz were back on the speedboat, speeding toward Academy Island.

"So what now?" Jaden asked.

"Now ye begin yer new life under the sea, Jaden," the Admiral said. He turned to the crew. "Sheets to the wind! We be makin' way to me first mate's new home!"

‹ • CHAPTER SIX • ›

FRIENDS TO THE END

Syrus sat on the dock, looking sadly out over the sea. "Jaden," he sighed, his voice forlorn.

Alexis and Chumley stood behind him, distressed.

"He's still waiting," Chumley said. "It's been a whole week since Jaden left."

"I guess that Jaden's made better friends," Syrus said. "Found himself a new crew."

"Syrus," Alexis said gently. "It's tough. I'm as upset as you are. But the Admiral said that Jaden wanted to stay. I guess for the money."

Suddenly, Syrus perked up. "Wait! You hear that?"

A speedboat appeared on the horizon.

"Syrus!" a voice called from the boat.

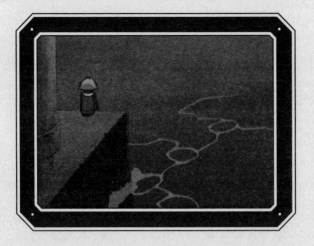

"Jaden?!" Syrus couldn't believe it.

"I escaped, Sy!" Jaden called out.

Black smoke billowed from the boat's motor. It sputtered and then stopped.

"Uh-oh. This doesn't look good," Jaden said.

Syrus jumped off the dock. "I'm coming, Jaden! I'll save you!" Syrus paddled toward the boat. "Jaden! I'm sorry! I want you to be my roommate again!"

"Really?" Jaden asked. "That's good to know. Because that weird admiral guy? Couldn't understand a word he said!"

"So we're cool?" Syrus asked.

"Of course!" Jaden said. "But, Sy, when'd you learn to swim?"

"Huh?" Syrus asked. He looked down at the water. "I didn't!" He began to splash around in the water.

Now Jaden jumped in to save Syrus.

"Syrus, grab me!" he called out.

"Only if you promise to get me a new bed!" Syrus answered.

"Okay," Jaden said. "But definitely not a water bed!"

• CHAPTER SEVEN •

DETECTIVE ZALOOG

A few days after Jaden escaped from the Admiral, he went to the health center to find Alexis. Chazz and Professor Banner went with him — along with a stranger to Academy Island.

Jaden found Alexis in the hall. Her brother, Atticus, looked out the large window at Academy Island, his eyes blank and distant. When Jaden had first met Atticus, he was the masked Shadow Rider known as Nightshroud. Losing the duel to Jaden had freed Atticus of the evil hold of the shadow world, but he hadn't been the same since.

"What's up, Alexis?" Jaden asked. "How's your bro Atticus doing?"

"So-so," Alexis said sadly. "I mean, he's out of that hospital bed now, but he still can't remember much of what happened."

"I'm sure he'll come around soon, Alexis," Jaden reassured her.

Alexis smiled gratefully. "Anyway, what brings you all over?"

"The law, actually," Professor Banner said.

The stranger stepped around the corner. He wore a tan jacket over a white shirt, and a tan cap on his head. He would have looked quite normal if it weren't for the strange eye patch over his right eye. It looked to be made of metal, and an Egyptian-looking eye was carved into it.

"Good afternoon, ma'am," the stranger said, taking off his cap. "I'm Detective Zaloog."

Professor Banner stroked his cat, Pharaoh, which he carried with him everywhere. "You see, Alexis, since

three of the seven Spirit Keys have already been taken by the Shadow Riders and the fate of the remaining world rests on protecting the remaining four, the academy thought it best to call in the police," he explained.

"By the way, where is your key, Lex?" Jaden asked.

"Right here, around my neck," Alexis answered.

Chazz nodded. "Same here."

"Same with me," Jaden added. All of the Key Keepers had hung the keys on strings and worn them around their necks, to keep them safe.

"Oh my," said the detective. "That's exactly what I was afraid of. You may think that's where it's safest, but it's not. All the Shadow Duelists have to do is find you, and then they've found the keys!"

"So, the detective suggests we hide our keys somewhere," Professor Banner said.

They all went to Chazz's room in the Slifer Red dorm first. Chazz was once a top student at Duel Academy, and had lived in the luxurious Obelisk Blue dorm. But he had left the academy for a while, and when he came back he had to start from the bottom — in the attic of Slifer Red.

Chazz hid his key in a storage cabinet.

"Just be sure that you keep it a secret," Detective Zaloog said.

Then the detective looked up. A tall man with a scar on his face stood outside the open door. He was painting a railing on the outside of the dorm.

"Who's that?" the detective asked.

"Oh, that's just Gorg. He's the janitor," Jaden explained.

Next they went to Jaden's room. He hid his key in the junk-filled drawer of his desk.

Just then, they heard the doorknob rattle. Jaden quickly walked to the door. He saw a short boy in a Slifer Red uniform standing there.

Syrus and Chumley walked up.

"Hey, CK, you lost again?" Syrus asked.

The nervous boy nodded and ran away.

"CK's a new exchange student," Chumley explained. "He's kinda on the slow side. I love dueling him!"

The next stop was Alexis's room in the Obelisk Blue dorm. As she hid the key in her jewelry box, a pretty woman in a white uniform stepped into the room.

"Who is this?" the detective asked suspiciously.

"She's just the school nurse," Alexis explained.

The nurse apologized for disturbing them and left.

Finally, they all went to Professor Banner's office. He put the key in his safe.

Detective Zaloog saw a man in a blue uniform walk past the office door.

"Wait! Who's that over there?" he asked.

"Oh, that's just Cliff, the security guard," Banner told him.

Outside the office window, the moon was rising over the horizon. Professor Banner yawned.

"Well, I guess we can all sleep soundly now," he said.

"Yes, quite soundly now," Detective Zaloog said. "Get to bed. You all must be exhausted."

So the Key Keepers went back to their rooms and slept. But while they did . . .

. . . someone drilled through the cabinet in Chazz's room.

. . . someone else pounded a hole through the wall of Jaden's room.

. . . a thick whip snaked out of an opening in the ceiling in Alexis's room. The whip curled around the jewelry box and carried it off.

. . . a gloved hand opened the safe in Professor Banner's office.

Deep beneath Academy Island, five mysterious figures gathered around the Spirit Gates. They were all that kept the world safe from the Sacred Beasts. The locks to the gates were centered on top of a large stone pillar. Three of the gates had already been opened by the Shadow Riders. Four remained.

"And it's done. All the Spirit Keys are ours," a voice said in the darkness.

"So why aren't the gates opening?" asked a female voice.

"We must have to do something else," said a boy's voice.

"And I'll bet those children know what that is," said the first voice angrily. "So much for doing this the nice way!"

• CHAPTER EIGHT •

DETECTIVE CHAZZ

The moon shone brightly in the sky as Jaden and Syrus raced to Chazz's room. They found Chazz in bed and started talking frantically. Chazz sat up and removed the earplugs from his ears.

"Uh, morons? See these little things in my ears? They're earplugs — now start over!" Chazz said.

"Your key!" Jaden cried. "It's vanished, Chazz! Look!"

Jaden pointed, and Chazz saw that his door had been broken down. He jumped out of bed and rushed to the storage cabinet. The door was in splinters — and the key was gone.

"It can't be!" Chazz exclaimed. "How?"

"Those things in your ears — they make it so you can't

39

hear doors being kicked in," Jaden said. "It looks like they're back."

Chazz's face clouded. "The Shadow Riders."

"Come on, we have to tell everyone!" Jaden said.

Moments later, Chazz's room was crowded with the remaining Key Keepers and their friends: Jaden, Syrus, Alexis, Professor Banner, and Chumley all sat on Chazz's large bed.

"So all of your keys are gone, too?" Chazz asked.

"Yes, I'm afraid so," Banner said.

"See, Jaden! *They* weren't wearing earplugs," Chazz pointed out.

"We'll figure this out!" a voice said from the doorway.

The friends looked up to see Detective Zaloog standing there, with four people behind him: the janitor, the school nurse, the security guard, and the exchange student — four people who had been around when the keys were hidden.

"I rounded up some suspects," Detective Zaloog

explained. "To help get to the bottom of this most serious crime."

"So you'll question them?" Banner asked.

"In due time," the detective said. "After I pose a few questions to you first."

Chazz frowned. "Something's up," he said suspiciously.

"Chazz, just let him do his job," Professor Banner scolded.

"Sorry," Chazz said dramatically. "But this is a job for . . . Chazz Princeton!" Chazz looked thoughtful as he made his case. "Everyone who knew where those keys were is in this room. So that means the thief has to be, too!"

"I guess," Syrus agreed. "But how will we find him? Won't we need evidence?"

"You know, I did see a press-on nail on my bedroom floor," Alexis offered.

The school nurse quickly hid one of her hands.

"A press-on nail? Sounds like a promising clue, Lex. So where is this press-on nail now?" Chazz asked.

Alexis blushed. "I, uh, kind of threw it in the garbage," she said sheepishly.

"I've got one!" Professor Banner said. "There was a set of footprints leading right up to my safe."

The security guard looked down at his shoes.

"That's perfect, Professor Banner," Chazz said eagerly. "What size shoe was it? What was the style of the shoe tread?"

Banner shrugged. "I, uh, kind of vacuumed them up."

"Ya know, there was a hole in the wall of our room," Jaden brought up.

CK the exchange student whistled and looked the other way.

"And let me guess, slacker," Chazz said. "You've already sealed it back up."

Jaden nodded his head. "Well, uh, kind of."

"You guys are really something," Chazz said, annoyed.

"Well, without any evidence, I guess we won't know who did it," Professor Banner remarked.

But Chazz had another idea. He stood up and pointed at the security guard. "He did it!" Chazz cried.

Everyone gasped.

"And him!" Chazz pointed at the exchange student.

"And him!" Chazz pointed at the big janitor.

"And her!" Chazz pointed at the school nurse.

CK the exchange student challenged Chazz. "You're basing this on what?"

"Yeah! You heard everyone! There's no proof," the school nurse pointed out.

"Oh, isn't there?" Chazz said. "How about we hear from them!"

Chazz held up three cards: Ojama Yellow, Ojama Green, and Ojama Black. Each card showed a different, strange-looking little creature.

"When we hid each of the Spirit Keys, I hid one of these cards with them," Chazz said. "The three of them are kind of my eyes and ears when I'm not around. And in my dorm room, I had all of these watching you!"

Chazz tried to skillfully fan out his deck of Duel Monsters cards, but the deck slipped from his hands and the cards fell on the bed. Chazz quickly scooped them up.

"The point is, they all saw who did it!" Chazz said.

The spirits of the three cards floated out in front of Chazz. Each monster wore a tiny red bathing suit. They all started talking at once.

"Caught ya red-handed!" said Ojama Black, a chubby creature with a big nose.

"*Soitenly* did!" said Ojama Green, a creature with one big eye and an even bigger mouth.

"You're so busted!" said Ojama Yellow. Two long eyestalks grew from the top of its yellow head.

Chazz smiled, triumphant. But he forgot one thing. Only he could see the spirits of the cards. They appeared to him because they had a bond together.

"Where are these so-called witnesses?" asked the school nurse.

"Well, maybe you can't see them, but I can," said Chazz. "And I know they're behind this, detective."

Detective Zaloog chuckled. "You're mistaken," he said. "It's not just them. It's me, too!"

"What!?" everyone cried at once.

"That's right, my children," said Zaloog. "All of us are in on it. We are the criminal ring known as . . . the Dark Scorpions!"

Zaloog and the four suspects took off their costumes. Underneath they wore brown and red matching uniforms. Each one carried a different weapon.

"Sorry, never heard of you," Jaden said.

"Of course you haven't," snapped Zaloog. "We've been deep undercover at your school for years now, waiting for our chance to nab those keys!"

"And now, the Scorpions finally have them!" the Scorpions all said together.

"So? To use them, you still have to beat me in a duel," Chazz said. "Bring it on!"

"Why you? I'll duel," Jaden offered.

"I'll take them on," Alexis said.

Chazz grunted. He wanted to face the Dark Scorpions himself.

"Or Professor Banner could," Syrus suggested.

The professor scooted back on the bed. "Oh, I'll sit this one out."

"That's it!" Zaloog cried. "Why the keys didn't work! We have to beat them in a duel!"

Chazz stepped forward. "Got that right! So let's go, Shadow Rider!"

◆ CHAPTER NINE ◆

MUSTERING OF THE DARK SCORPIONS

Chazz and Zaloog walked outside the Slifer Red dorm and faced off under the moonlight. The Dark Scorpions all stood behind Zaloog, and Chazz's friends stood behind him. Both duelists activated their Duel Disks.

"Duel!" they cried.

"I'll win this as easily as I stole your keys," Zaloog said confidently. "First I'll summon Golem Sentry in defense mode."

A monster that looked like a flat, stone wall with a battle-axe across it appeared in front of Zaloog.

"That'll do for now," the Dark Scorpion said.

"My turn!" Chazz shouted. "I play the spell card Fiend's Sanctuary!"

He held up a card with a picture of a gargoyle on it.

"With this card, I can summon a Metal Fiend Token to the field," Chazz said. A token made of silver metal appeared. "And now, I'll sacrifice my Fiend Token to bring out Armed Dragon Level Five!"

The Fiend Token screeched and vanished in a flash. In its place stood a sturdy red and black dragon with a barrel-shaped body. Spiked armor covered its arms and chest, and it had 2400 attack points.

"Go, Armed Dragon!" Chazz called out. "Use those arms to destroy that Golem. Spiked Spinner!"

The dragon's two spiked arms began to spin, turning them into dangerous weapons. It rushed across the field and tore at Golem Sentry, sending pieces of stone flying across the field. Zaloog's monster was decimated. Zaloog groaned.

"For my next move, I'm gonna place two facedowns," Chazz continued. "Then I'll use my dragon's ability — and it's a big one!"

Everyone gasped as Chazz put Armed Dragon Level 5 back in his deck. He pulled another card, and a bigger, stronger-looking dragon appeared—with 2800 attack points!

"On the turn that Armed Dragon Level Five wins a fight, you can trade him in for a Level Seven!" Chazz bragged.

Zaloog's face turned grim. "Level him up all you want. It won't matter!" he said. "And you're about to see why."

He held up a card. "First, I play Pot of Greed! It lets me draw two more cards from my deck." Zaloog drew two cards and smiled. "Just what I wanted. The one and only Don Zaloog!"

He held up a card, and the picture on it looked exactly like him!

"And when I say one and only, I really mean it," Zaloog said, stepping forward with 1400 attack points. "Because, my children, I *am* him!"

On the sidelines, Syrus scratched his head, confused. "Wait, so . . ."

"He's a card!" Chumley exclaimed.

Jaden shook his head. "Whoa!" How could a duelist and a card be one and the same?

"And it's not just me," Zaloog went on. He held up another card. "With Mustering of the Dark Scorpions, I can summon all of them. That's right! All the Dark Scorpions in my hand — come join me on the field!"

The four Scorpions ran up next to Don Zaloog — the big, muscled man with the scar on his face; the pretty woman who had posed as the school nurse; the short kid; and the slim guy who had pretended to be a security guard. But now they all wore their brown and red uniforms.

"Now, Scorpions, roll call!" Don Zaloog cried.

The big guy with the scarred face looked confused. "Rolls? Where are da rolls?" He had 1800 attack points and carried a mace, a staff with a spiked ball on the end.

"He means say your name, Gorg," said the woman. She held a nasty-looking whip, and boasted 1000 attack points. "I'm Meanae the Thorn."

The former security guard held a dangerous-looking knife in front of him and packed a whopping 1200 attack points. "The name's Cliff the Trap Remover," he said, grinning. "Guess how I remove 'em!"

The blond-haired boy had a large mallet and 1000 attack points. He began to jump up and down. "I'm Chick the Yellow," he said, "and I'm six foot — when I jump up!"

"And together, we're the Dark Scorpions!" all five cried at once.

Chazz's steely gray eyes did not show any fear. "Losers," he said.

"Now I'll play a trap!" Don Zaloog said. "You see, on the first turn that all the Dark Scorpions are out, this trap allows each of us to attack you directly. And for every one of those attacks, you lose 400 life points!"

Don Zaloog turned to his teammates. "Now let him have it. Dark Scorpion Combination!"

Meanae moved first, lashing at Chazz with her whip. "Take this! Thorn Whip!"

"Double Blast Attack!" Don Zaloog yelled, pummeling Chazz with two weapons.

Cliff the Trap Remover slashed at Chazz with his knife. "Scorpion Slice!"

Chick the Yellow leapt up. "Mallet Mash!" he yelled, pounding Chazz.

"Hammer! Hammer!" Gorg finished the job with his heavy mace.

Chazz's friends watched, worried, as a cloud of dust rose up around Chazz, stirred up by the attack. When the dust cleared, Chazz was pale and sweating. His life points dropped from 4000 down to 2000.

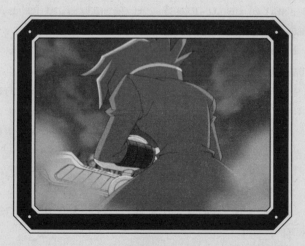

"This isn't how you want to start a duel!" Jaden called out.

Chazz struggled to catch his breath. Don Zaloog grinned, pleased.

"There's more, too. For you see, Chazz, now our special abilities go into effect against you," he said.

"Say what?" Chazz yelped. How could there be more punishment than what he'd already been through?

"That's right. First a monster on your field must return to the top of your deck," Gorg the Strong said. Armed Dragon Level 7 disappeared.

"And then next, a card on your field returns to your hand," Chick the Yellow added. One of Chazz's facedowns jumped into his hand. Chazz gave an angry grunt.

"There's more!" said Cliff the Trap Remover. "The top two cards on your deck? They go to the grave!"

Chazz gritted his teeth as his top two cards, including his mighty Armed Dragon, went to the graveyard.

"And then one card in your hand is destroyed!" Zaloog said.

Chazz held back anger as a card in his hand disappeared.

But the Dark Scorpions still weren't finished.

"And finally, a card with Dark Scorpion in its name can be added to *our* hand from the graveyard," Meanae said.

"And I'll pick this," Don Zaloog jumped in. "Dark Scorpion Combination! The card that started it all!"

His one eye glared at Chazz with an evil glint.

"And now, I'll end it all!"

• CHAPTER TEN •

OJAMA TRIO TO THE RESCUE!

"Stay tough, Chazz!" Jaden called out. "You can beat these guys!"

"Hel-lo," Chazz said sarcastically. "Of course I can! Now be quiet, and let the Chazz do his thing."

Chazz held up a card. "I play Level Modulation," he announced. "Now you get to draw two cards, and I get to summon from the grave a high-level monster — without paying a dime!"

Chazz took a card from his graveyard.

"I choose Armed Dragon Level Seven!" Chazz cried.

A red light flashed on the field as the massive dragon appeared.

"Him again?" Zaloog asked, annoyed. He drew his

two cards. "You give me no choice but to play two face-downs, then."

Syrus watched nervously from the side. "I hate it when this guy plays facedowns."

"I hear ya, Syrus," Jaden agreed. "This should be interesting."

"It's my turn!" Chazz reminded Zaloog. "And first, Armed Dragon Level Seven's effect activates. Now by sending one monster card in my hand to the grave, monsters with attack points equal to or fewer than my discarded one are destroyed!"

The Dark Scorpions exchanged worried glances. Depending on what monster Chazz chose, they could all end up in the graveyard.

"The card I'm discarding is Despair from the Dark!" Chazz held up the card. "2800 attack points!"

But Zaloog had a strategy.

"Hold it!" he yelled. "I play a trap! Retreat of the Dark Scorpions! Now all Dark Scorpions on the field retreat to my hand!"

The Dark Scorpions, including Don Zaloog, ran off the field.

"Fine, I'll attack directly," Chazz said. "Armed Dragon, go get him! Dragon Sonic Sphere!"

Armed Dragon opened his claw. A pulsating ball of energy formed there. He hurled the ball at Don Zaloog. *Slam!* The duelist reeled from the attack.

"Oh no!" the other Dark Scorpions yelled.

"How dare he strike the boss like that!" Cliff said.

"Don't worry," Meanae said darkly. "We'll get him back."

Chazz grinned smugly. "I place one card facedown and end my turn!"

Don Zaloog snorted. "One lucky move, that's all! But it won't matter. It ends here! I summon myself, Don Zaloog, again!"

He stepped back out onto the field.

"Then I'll play Mustering of the Dark Scorpions!" he announced. "Welcome back, team!"

But before the Dark Scorpions could step back on the field, Chazz held up a card.

"Sorry, they're not back yet," he said. "I play Ojama Trio!"

Ojama Yellow, Ojama Black, and Ojama Green appeared on the field — in front of Don Zaloog!

"Hey, why are they on our field?" Cliff asked.

"So that you can't be!" Chazz shot back. "See, Ojama Trio creates Ojama Tokens, and they take up three of your monster slots. When destroyed, you lose 300 life points!"

Ojama Black rolled in the dirt. "Sorry, pal!" he told Don Zaloog.

"Thanks for havin' us," said Ojama Green, giggling.

Ojama Yellow rocked back and forth and sipped from a yellow mug. "I just love hot chocolate!"

"So we can't come out? No fair!" Chick the Yellow whined.

But there was room on the field for one more monster.

"I can!" Meanae said. "Go on, boss! Do what you have to do."

"Meanae, I'll never forget you for this," Zaloog said. He held up a card. "I play Dark Scorpion–Tragedy of Love. When Don Zaloog and Meanae the Thorn are on the field, I can send Meanae to the graveyard to destroy *all* of your monsters!"

Meanae leapt through the air, brandishing her whip.

She lashed out at Armed Dragon Level 7. The dragon shattered.

"Avenge me, boss! Avenge me!" she cried, her voice full of despair. Then she vanished.

Don Zaloog and Chazz glared at each other across the field.

"I attack you directly!" Don Zaloog called out. "Double Blast Attack!"

Zaloog attacked Chazz, and his life points dropped down to 600. Chazz groaned, trying not to show the pain on his face.

"And now my special ability activates!" Don Zaloog said. "You have to discard one random card from your hand!"

Chazz raised his head. A small smile appeared on his face.

"Actually," he said, "it would be my pleasure!"

• CHAPTER ELEVEN •

HAIL, OJAMA KING!

"The only card in my hand is Ojama Magic," Chazz announced. "And when this card is sent to the graveyard, well then . . . Ojama Yellow, Green, and Black all come to my hand."

The Ojama Trio happily hopped across the field. But the three Ojama Tokens created in the last move stayed with Don Zaloog.

"Bring 'em out!" Zaloog challenged. "They don't scare me!"

"Yeah, well, we'll see what I can do to change that," Chazz said. "My turn! Go, Pot of Greed!"

Chazz took two cards from his Duel Disk. He held up one of the cards. "Next, I play Polymerization. Scared yet?"

Zaloog grunted. Whatever was coming, it couldn't be good.

"Do your thing, Ojamas!" Chazz yelled.

The Ojama Trio happily jumped in the air, ready to fuse into a new monster.

"You got it!' said Ojama Yellow.

"Time to show these numbskulls!" said Ojama Black.

"It *soitenly* is!" added Ojama Green.

Colorful bands of light flashed around them as they swirled around in the sky. Then a huge creature appeared in their place. It had a huge round head, a fleshy body, and its eyes looked out from two long eyestalks.

"Ojama King!" it boomed.

The Ojama Tokens cheered. "Yeah! Hail to the king!"

"What is this?" Don Zaloog wondered.

Ojama King had zero attack points, but Chazz didn't seem to be worried about that.

"Now I'll play my spell card," Chazz continued. "Ojamuscle!"

Ojama King grunted as bulging muscles burst out all over his body. His eyestalks sought out the Ojama Tokens on the field.

"Ojama Tokens, come to Daddy!" he cried.

He opened his mouth and a long, gray tongue snaked out. The tongue scooped up the three cheering Ojama Tokens and took them into Ojama King's massive mouth. The monster swallowed them in one gulp.

"Ojamuscle destroys all Ojama monsters out, and for every one that's destroyed, King gains one thousand attack points," Chazz explained. "Oh, and since those were Ojama *Tokens* that were destroyed, you now lose 900 life points!"

Zaloog grunted as his life points dropped down to 300.

"And now, King's attack points will rise to three thousand!" Chazz said. Ojama King's big belly jiggled as he chuckled happily.

"Now go, Ojama King!" Chazz cried. "Attack Don with Flying Belly Flop Drop!"

A look of pure fear crossed Zaloog's face as the huge Ojama King jumped up in the air. It held its arms out like it was jumping off of a diving board. Then it plummeted down toward Don Zaloog.

"Incoming!" Ojama King yelled.

He fell . . . and fell . . . and . . . *WHAM!*

Don Zaloog was crushed under the weight of the humongous monster.

"All right!" Syrus cheered.

"You won!" Chumley said.

"Way to duel, Chazz!" Jaden added.

Ojama King bounced off of Don Zaloog. Chazz stood over him.

"Bye-bye," he said.

"No, this can't be!" Don Zaloog said. "We can't lose!"

The Dark Scorpions ran toward their boss. But there was nothing they could do. A bright light burned from inside all of them. The light flashed.

All five Scorpions were gone. All that remained of Don Zaloog was his metal eye patch. A Duel Monsters card fluttered to the ground, and Chazz picked it up. The card showed all five Dark Scorpions. They were trapped inside the card now.

"Well, guys, guess that's one less Shadow Rider we have to worry about," Chazz said, looking at the card thoughtfully.

"Yes, and now the Spirit Keys are back in safe hands," Professor Banner said.

"But where's Don Zaloog? And the other Scorpions?" Alexis asked.

"Don't know," Jaden said. "But Chazz seems concerned."

Everyone headed back to bed. Chazz put in his earplugs once again — but as he suspected, they didn't do much good.

The spirits of Ojama Trio came out of their cards, just like they always did. But this time, they had company. The spirits of all five Dark Scorpions joined them!

"You sure know how to throw a good party, Ojama Yellow," said Don Zaloog.

"Hey, where's Ojama King?" asked Meanae.

"He comes late — he likes to make a big entrance!" Ojama Yellow answered.

Chazz sighed and rolled over.

Saving the Spirit Keys felt pretty good. But a good night's sleep would be even better!

• CHAPTER TWELVE •

LEGENDARY DUELISTS

The Duel Academy students in Professor Banner's class were all awake and interested — even Jaden, for once. The professor was giving a lecture on legendary duelists.

Two sketched portraits appeared on the big screen behind Banner's desk.

"You all know Yugi Moto and Seto Kaiba as dueling legends," the professor said. "Far and away the very best of their generation!"

The class whispered excitedly at the sight of the two duelists.

"They're total dreamboats," sighed one girl from the Obelisk Blue dorm.

"I like Mai Valentine," said a boy in a red Slifer uniform.

"But you do realize, class, that there were other great duelists well before all of them," Banner continued.

"How is that, prof?" Jaden asked. "I mean, Duel Monsters hasn't been around all that long."

"Guess you were asleep during that class, Jaden," Syrus told him. "They used to play back in ancient Egypt!"

"That's right," Banner agreed. "And one of the best way back in those days was a powerful pharaoh named Abidos the Third. He was undefeated."

A picture of the pharaoh appeared on the screen.

"Undefeated? That's so sweet!" Jaden said, impressed. "He must've been something else! Of course it's a good thing he's not around today, cause then that unde-feated record would go adios!"

Chazz sat right behind Jaden. He shook his head at Jaden's bragging.

"*Sure* it would, slacker," Chazz said. "Then you'd probably take down Yugi and Kaiba, too!

"Ya think?" Jaden asked. "Well, thanks! I had no idea you believed in me so much, Chazz."

"It's *sarcasm*," Chazz fumed. "Got that?"

"Sure," Jaden said, still smiling. "But if you want to change your name, Chazz, you can do a lot better than 'sarcasm.'"

"You know what I mean!" Frustrated, Chazz began to shake Jaden's shoulders. Jaden laughed.

"Hey, come on guys," Syrus warned. "You're going to get us in trouble!"

"Wanna see trouble?" Chazz asked. "How about this?" He pulled on Jaden's ears.

"Stop!" Syrus cried. "He's going to hear us!"

"He sure will."

The boys looked to see the professor hovering over them.

"You can continue in detention," he said firmly.

Syrus groaned. "Oh, man. Fifth time this week!

• CHAPTER THIRTEEN •

MUMMIES!

Later that day, Alexis stood with Syrus's brother, Zane, at the base of one of the island's lighthouses. The sun had already set, and the beams from the lighthouse shone above them. They lit up the black waves that lapped against the island's shore.

"Thanks for coming," Alexis told Zane. "I just needed someone to talk to."

Zane nodded. He might have been Syrus's brother, but they couldn't be more different. Syrus was short with unruly hair and glasses. Zane was tall and good-looking with wavy hair that never fell out of place.

"I thought having my brother Atticus back would make everything okay," Alexis continued. "But it seems like there are more questions than ever now. And then with these Shadow Riders . . ."

"But right now we're safe, Alexis," Zane assured her.

"Yeah . . ." Alexis's voice trailed off. The waves around the base of the lighthouse suddenly began to swell. They crashed against the stone base.

At the same time, the base began to shake violently.

Alexis and Zane gasped. Creatures rose from the rubble, as though they had been buried. Their bodies were wrapped in filthy cloth, and their eyes grinned evilly from behind their bandages.

Alexis wanted to scream, but she couldn't get the words out.

Mummies!

On a pathway above the lighthouse, Jaden, Syrus, and Chazz walked back to their dorm.

"I spend more time in detention that I do in class," Syrus complained. "My mom's not going to be happy." He sighed. "At least things can't get worse!"

Aaaaaaaaiiiiieeeeeeeeee! Alexis's screams pierced through the night.

"What was that?" Jaden asked. He peered over the edge of the path. Light from the lighthouse showed an eerie scene. Alexis and Zane — facing off against a group of mummies!

Jaden, Syrus, and Chazz ran down to the water's edge.

"Save yourselves!" Zane cried out.

"No way!" Jaden said, panting as he ran. "You need help!"

One of the mummies turned to Jaden. "Give . . . us . . . the . . . Spirit Key."

Jaden looked down at the key that hung around his neck. "My key?"

"Shadow Riders!" Chazz exclaimed.

Jaden took a step forward, ready to face the mummies. Then a blinding light stopped him. He covered his face with his arms.

He looked up and squinted to see a strange craft in the sky — it looked like some kind of golden spaceship. A voice thundered from the craft.

"Duelists, I have come for you!" the voice cried.

Then Jaden's world went black.

• CHAPTER FOURTEEN •

THE PHARAOH ABIDOS

Jaden's eyes fluttered opened. Everything looked blurry. Then he heard a familiar voice.

"Welcome back, Jaden."

It was Zane. His friend's face came into focus, and he saw that all his friends were there . . . plus one more.

"Professor Banner?" Jaden asked.

"Those mummies found me and brought me here," the professor replied. His cat, Pharaoh, was curled up in his lap. "That Spirit Key must have led them to me."

"That must be how they found all of us," Zane mused.

Jaden jumped to his feet. The mummies had to be nearby. But where were they, exactly? The ground underneath him looked like it was made of solid gold. Had they been transported to that weird ship in the sky?

He ran to a golden wall and looked over the edge. The others followed him. They all gasped at the sight before them.

A man wearing the costume of an Egyptian pharaoh sat on a golden throne, flanked by servants. His dark eyes shone from the gold mask that covered his face, and gold bracelets circled his arms.

"Hello there," the pharaoh said calmly.

Professor Banner fainted, falling onto his back. Pharaoh jumped up on his chest and licked his face, concerned.

"What's wrong with him?" Syrus asked.

"I don't know," Chazz replied. "Looks like he's seen a ghost."

Jaden scrambled across the wall and found himself on a dueling platform. He charged toward the pharaoh.

"What's the big idea?" he shouted angrily.

"That's not how one should address an Egyptian pharaoh," the masked man said.

"He looked just like the picture Banner showed us in class today," Chazz remarked.

"Abidos," Alexis said.

"He's a Shadow Rider," Zane said firmly. "He's after those Sacred Beasts, just like all the rest of them!"

Chazz looked at the pharaoh's servants, masked men who all carried long spears. "It seems like the punk's got us outnumbered!" he cried.

"That's right," Abidos said. "So just leave your keys and walk away. You don't want to duel me!"

Jaden waved his hand like a kid in school. "I do! Over here! Pick me! Pick me!"

"Jaden!" Syrus warned.

But Jaden ignored his friend. "Let me show you how we duel in the twenty-first century," he called out.

"You can't talk to me like that!" Abidos fumed.

"Jaden, you do realize this will be a Shadow Game," Zane said.

"He's right," Alexis said. "Your soul's on the line."

"And this guy's undefeated," Syrus added.

"Not for long," Jaden said confidently. "I mean, once I'm done with him, *I'll* be the legend. So get your game on!"

"My game is always on!" the pharaoh countered.

Chazz tossed a Duel Disk across the arena. He knew Abidos would need a modern disk to battle Jaden.

"Catch!" Chazz cried.

Syrus frowned. "Hey, that Duel Disk looks just like mine!"

Abidos caught the disk. Jaden faced him across the arena.

"Time to throw down!" Jaden challenged.

"Duel!" The two duelists cried at once.

They both activated their Duel Disks and drew their cards. Each one started out with 4000 life points.

Abidos examined his cards. "Let's see," he said. "First, I think I'll summon Pharaonic Protector in defense mode!"

He held up the card, and a masked servant appeared

on the field in a kneeling position. His defense points flashed in front of him: 0000.

"No defense points?" Syrus was shocked. Why would anyone play a monster in defense mode if it didn't have any defense points to absorb damage?

"Then I'll lay a facedown," Abidos said calmly. "Your turn."

"Then here I go!" Jaden cried.

"Not before I activate The First Sarcophagus," Abidos said.

"Huh?" Jaden asked. "Never heard of that card."

The pharaoh's facedown card rose up. It had a picture of a golden tomb filled with jewels on it.

"Well, after this match, you'll never forget it. Though you may want to," Abidos said. "But I'm afraid you'll have to wait until I bring out another *two* sarcophagi before you see why, Key Keeper."

The pharaoh's cryptic warnings didn't bother Jaden. "Okay, whatever," he said. "Can I go now? Because I've got a couple of Duel Monsters tricks of my own that I want to show you."

"Put your monsters where your mouth is," Abidos shot back.

"You asked for it!" Jaden said. "Here's Elemental Hero Avian in attack mode!"

Jaden's winged hero appeared on the field, with 1000 attack points flashing next to him.

"And check out this spell card," Jaden continued. A giant letter "H" appeared in front of the card and then faded away. "Heated Heart! Now a monster on my field gains five hundred extra attack points. Not too shabby, huh?"

Jaden grinned as Avian's attack points jumped to 1500.

"But there's more," he said. "If Avian attacks a monster in defense mode, the extra damage goes right to you! See for yourself. Quill Cascade!"

At Jaden's command, Avian let loose a barrage of

sharp feathers that shot across the dueling field like darts. The feathers assaulted Pharaonic Protector and then slammed into Abidos himself. He cried out in surprise, and his life points dropped down to 2500.

"Sweetness!" Jaden said. "Dueling's not what it used to be. Right, old timer?"

"No, dueling is much tamer now," Abidos sneered, shaking off the attack. "But let me give you a taste of the old school. I play Second Sarcophagus! And once the third card is played, the duel and your soul will be mine."

Another Sarcophagus card appeared on the field, flanking Abidos.

"What's it do?" Alexis wondered from the sidelines.

Syrus shuddered. "I don't want to know."

Abidos continued his turn. "Next I'll play Pot of Greed," he said. "This lets me draw two more cards from my deck. And I think I'll play one right now. Go, Tribute of the Doomed!"

Abidos held up the card, which showed a creepy mummy. "Now, by discarding one card from my hand, your Avian is destroyed!"

A chilly wind whipped up around Avian as the pharaoh moved one of his cards to the graveyard. A puddle of clay formed around Avian's feet, and two strong arms emerged from the clay and pulled Avian into the muck. Jaden's hero was gone!

"Next I'll play Pharaoh's Servant in attack mode," Abidos said. "Now attack!"

A figure that looked just like one of the pharoah's masked servants appeared on the field. It charged right at Jaden, its long spear extended.

"Aaaaaah!" Jaden cried out as the force of the attack hit him. His life points dropped down to 3100.

"Jaden!" Syrus cried out.

"My undefeated record will be staying intact," Abidos said smugly. "But *you* will not!"

• CHAPTER FIFTEEN •

LEGEND OR LOSER?

"Don't worry, Key Keeper," Abidos taunted Jaden. "After I play this facedown, it's your turn again. *If* you have the strength left to play, that is."

Jaden stood straight up and looked Abidos directly in the eyes. "Come on," he said. "Give us present-day peeps some credit. It's my go — and I play Emergency Call!"

Jaden held up the card, and a green letter "E" appeared in front of him. "This card springs an Elemental Hero from my hand. And the hero I'm springing is going to be Sparkman!"

Jaden's blue and gold hero appeared in front of him. Lightning bolts flashed around Sparkman and his impressive 1600 attack points.

"And there's more," Jaden promised. "Now I'm play-ing the spell card known as Righteous Justice!"

A big letter "R" appeared and faded on the field.

"What's that do?" Syrus wondered.

"For every elemental hero that Jaden has out on his field, one of Abidos's trap or spell cards is destroyed," Zane explained.

"Yeah, like that First Sarcophagus card you got over there!" Jaden called out to Abidos. "Looks like we're not going to be seeing what it does after all!"

Abidos growled behind his mask.

"Righteous Justice, destroy the First Sarcophagus!" Jaden commanded. Rays of golden light reached out from the card, seeking their target.

"I don't think so!" Abidos said quickly. "Go, Magic Jammer! It turns your Righteous Justice into a righteous waste!"

Jaden frowned as purple smoke poured from Magic Jammer. The curling smoke obliterated the rays from

Righteous Justice, and the spell card's effect was stopped.

Still, Jaden was impressed with the pharaoh's move. "Wicked counter!" he admitted. "That's what I'm talking about!"

"You *should* be talking about getting some new cards for that weak deck," Abidos sneered.

On the sidelines, Syrus cringed at the comment. "Ooh, he shouldn't have said that," he said. He knew the more you taunted Jaden, the better duelist he became.

Alexis knew it, too. "Yeah, bad call," she agreed.

"Weak? See if you think this is weak!" Jaden called out to Abidos. "Sparkman, attack!"

Sparkman shot a blast of electric energy across the dueling field. Abidos whimpered as his life points dropped down to 1800. He seemed to be in total disbelief of what had happened.

"You . . . you can't attack me!" Abidos said.

Jaden pretended to be a little confused. "I can't?" he asked. "Hate to break it to you, but yeah, I can. That's how you play the game. Read the rule book!"

"But I am Abidos, the greatest duelist ever!" the pharaoh protested, his voice faltering.

"The greatest? Uh, I'm not so sure about that," Jaden said. "To tell you the truth, you haven't even been dueling that great. I mean for someone who's undefeated, I was hoping for . . . I don't know. Some super sweet monsters, or wicked rare cards! But so far, I've been kind of underwhelmed."

"Yeah, his cards are hardly better than a starter

deck," Syrus agreed. "For a legend, this guy is a bit of a letdown."

"Looks like Jaden's going to win this one easy," Chazz sighed. "There goes my shot at a new room."

The pharaoh didn't respond to Jaden's comments. Jaden waited for him to make a move, talk back, do something, but Abidos was silent. His dark eyes seemed distant.

Abidos thought back to the days spent in his kingdom, before his master from the Shadow Realm had transported him here. As a young pharaoh, he had dueled servant after servant, winning the duels each and every time.

But had he? Every victory had been so easy — too easy. And then there were the whispered words of the servants one afternoon. . . .

"*You know I'm getting tired of having to lose to this spoiled brat every time!*"

"*If we beat him, he'll probably feed us to the lions!*"

The realization slowly dawned on Abidos.

"Could it be my servants *let* me win?" he said out loud.

"Let you win?" Jaden couldn't believe it.

Chazz sneered on the sidelines. "Wow, what a giant loser this guy is."

"You know, I wouldn't mind having servants like that," Syrus said.

"But his whole life has been a lie!" Alexis pointed out.

Jaden shook his head. "So you never *really* dueled before?"

"I guess not," Abidos said. He sounded sad and defeated.

Jaden smiled. "Then let's start your first lesson right now!"

"What?" Abidos was startled.

"You heard me right. Now get your game on . . . again!" Jaden cried. "But if this is going to be your first real duel, let's do this right and ditch that mask."

Abidos slowly removed the mask to reveal the tanned face of a young pharaoh. He didn't appear to be much older than Zane.

"Jaden, just promise me you'll give your best," Abidos said.

"That's all I ever give!" Jaden said. "Now let's duel!"

Abidos actually smiled, excited to be in his first real duel. But Jaden still had to finish his move.

"I'm throwing down a facedown," Jaden said. "All right, Abidos. Your move!"

"Very well," Abidos said. "I activate Third Sarcophagus!"

Now the images of three cards with golden tombs floated next to the pharaoh.

"Leave it to Jaden to pep-talk a Shadow Rider," Alexis said. It looked like Abidos had a big move planned.

"And I sacrifice all three to finally summon Spirit of the Pharaoh in attack mode!" Abidos announced.

"Spirit of the who what?" Jaden was shocked.

The pharaoh's three Sarcophagus cards glowed, then vanished. In their place appeared a shining gold tomb at the pharaoh's feet. The lid of the sarcophagus slowly slid to the side, and a tall and muscled pharaoh stepped out, covered in blue and solid gold armor. A shimmering gold

mask covered the monster's face. 2500 attack points flashed next to him.

"Well, I guess he *looks* cool, but I've got to admit — I expected a whole lot more than 2500 attack points," Jaden remarked.

"I'm not done!" Abidos said, his eyes shining with new confidence. "A pharaoh is nothing without his servants. Whenever he's summoned, I get to call up his friends. Up to four level two zombies from my graveyard!"

Bright light flashed as two Pharaonic Protectors appeared back on the field. Then two Pharaoh's Servants materialized. Each servant had 900 attack points.

Jaden nodded. This was more like it.

"And now, my draw!" Abidos cried.

"Not so fast!" Jaden countered. "Go Invincible Hero!"

Jaden's facedown card flipped up to reveal a picture of a burly hero.

"For this one turn, you can't destroy my Sparkman," Jaden said.

"Then I suppose it's a very good thing I have this card," Abidos said, holding up a new card from his hand.

"Huh?" Jaden wondered. What did Abidos have planned?

"I activate the powers of Thousand Energy!" Abidos cried. "Now all my level two monsters on the field gain one thousand attack points!"

"Aw, man!" Syrus groaned.

"'Aw man' is right," Professor Banner agreed. "Because that is 300 more attack points than Jaden's Sparkman! Meaning the extra damage goes right to . . ."

"Jaden!" Syrus cried.

The four servants charged across the field, their spears extended. They slammed into Sparkman, then descended on Jaden.

"Sparkman may survive the battle, but Jaden still takes damage," Alexis explained. "Three hundred points for *each* of those zombies!"

"But that'll be like twelve hundred life points!" Syrus cried.

As he said it, Jaden's life points dropped down to 1900.

"There's more," Abidos said. "I still have Spirit Pharaoh himself! Attack!"

Spirit Pharaoh and Sparkman clashed in the center of the dueling arena. Sparkman absorbed most of the attack, but Jaden still took a hit. His life points dropped to 1000.

"Jay!" Syrus yelled.

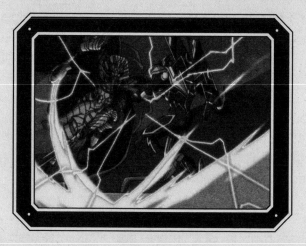

And Abidos still wasn't finished.

"Now I think I'll activate one of my monsters," Abidos said. "To activate a little card I like to call Soul Guide!"

One of the Pharaonic protectors vanished.

"It gives me life points equal to the attack points of the card I lost," Abidos explained, and his life points jumped to 3700 as he said it.

"But it's about to get a whole lot better," the pharaoh continued. "Soul Guide lets me put a copy of the card I just sacrificed right back in my hand! And even though Thousand Energy will most certainly destroy my monsters, from how your life points will turn out, it will be worth it!"

The Pharaonic Protector appeared, but then all four servants vanished — the cost of using Thousand Energy.

Abidos gleamed triumphantly.

"My undefeated record shall stand!"

⟨ • CHAPTER SIXTEEN • ⟩

HERO FLASH!

Abidos expected Jaden to quiver with fear. Instead, he saw Jaden grinning.

"What's so funny?" the pharaoh asked. "You're about to lose your soul!"

"Not yet!" Jaden replied.

Abidos raised an eyebrow. "Is that so?"

"That's right," Jaden said confidently. "And you're about to see why!"

Jaden drew a card and smiled.

"I summon Elemental Hero Clayman in attack mode!"

Jaden's rock-solid hero appeared and roared loudly. Clayman had 800 attack points.

"Then I'll play this card. It's called Oversoul," Jaden said.

Jaden held up the card, and a big letter "O" appeared, then faded.

"And boy is it sweet," Jaden continued. "I get to summon an Elemental Hero back from the graveyard and I think I know just the one. Elemental Hero Avian!"

A green-clad hero with huge white, feathered wings appeared, along with 1000 attack points.

Abidos just sneered. "So what? You've got three weak monsters. They can't beat my Pharaoh! He'll take them apart one at a time."

"Sorry, but he won't be getting the chance," Jaden said. "See, Abidos. Your three-card combo was pretty sweet. But I got a four card one. Heated Heart! Emergency Call! Righteous Justice! And last but not least, Oversoul!"

As Jaden spoke, glowing letters emerged from the cards and appeared in front of him. They spelled out HERO!

"Together, they're activating this — the one and only spell card known as Hero Flash!" Jaden cried.

"Never heard of it," Abidos scoffed.

"Well, you're never gonna forget it," Jaden promised him. "First, I get to summon Elemental Hero Burstinatrix from my deck in attack mode!"

Fiery Burstinatrix joined the other heroes lined up in front of Jaden. She added 1200 attack points to the mix.

"But that's not all, Abidos," Jaden continued. "Now all the heroes I have out get to attack your life points directly!"

Abidos gasped.

"Now Elemental Heroes, let's put a blemish on that perfect record of his!" Jaden cried. "Hero Flash!"

The four heroes joined forces, letting out a loud bat-

tle cry. A wave of rainbow-colored light emerged from their bodies and streamed across the field. The light swallowed up both Abidos and his Spirit Pharaoh.

When the light faded, Spirit Pharaoh was gone. Abidos was on his knees, and his life points were totally wiped out.

"That's game!" Jaden cheered. "And a pretty good one, too! You got moves."

"Yeah, but not like Jaden's," Alexis remarked.

"Big fat hairy deal," Chazz said. "Ojama Hurricane's just as good."

"Abidos doesn't look so good," Syrus said.

Jaden looked at the fallen pharaoh. "Hey, what's the matter?"

Abidos sighed. "I used to think I was the best duelist of all time. But now I know. I need a lot of practice if I want to be a true dueling legend."

"Hey, any time!" Jaden said cheerfully.

Abidos brightened. "Well, I was thinking right now."

"Right now? You want a rematch?" Jaden asked.

"No," Abidos said. "You could come back with me!"

"Jaden?" Syrus was worried. Would he lose his friend to this pharaoh?

"You're too good for this place," Abidos told Jaden.

"Come back to my kingdom and I promise you fame and power!"

"Uh, nice offer," Jaden said. "But I think I prefer it right here. Drop me a line if you're ever in my hood, okay?"

"Same with you," Abidos said. "That is, if you ever find a time vortex warping loop hole . . ."

Suddenly, Jaden and his friends found themselves back on the grounds of Academy Island. Abidos and his servants were above them now, standing on the gold spaceship.

"You know what? I'll just call you," Abidos said. "Farewell!"

Then the ship rose up into the night sky and vanished.

Jaden thought about the duel as he and his friends walked back to their dorms.

"You know, Abidos wasn't such a bad guy," Jaden said. "I mean, look what he gave me!"

Jaden twirled a gold Egyptian bracelet around his arm. Every time he won a Shadow Duel, he earned some kind of prize from the loser.

"I'm starting to get quite a collection," he kidded. "But where's the Shadow Rider with the skateboard?"

"I don't see why Jaden gets all the free stuff," Chazz mumbled.

"Probably because I beat a dueling legend," Jaden said.

"Oh, *now* he's a legend? Cause you beat him?" Chazz snapped.

"Well, Chazz, that *is* what the history books say he is. Right?" Syrus said.

Chazz frowned. "Well, we know the truth. He was a sham! A fake!"

"Jaden the legend slayer! I like the sound of that," Jaden said.

Behind him, Professor Banner stopped. He studied Jaden carefully, a serious expression on his face.

"Good, Jaden, because soon you will get the chance to truly earn it," the professor said softly. "Soon you will face . . . your true test!"